This Walker book belongs to:

_____

_____

_____

For Emily and Giles Woolley

First published 1985 by Walker Books Ltd
87 Vauxhall Walk, London SE11 5HJ

This edition published 2016

2 4 6 8 10 9 7 5 3 1

© 1985 Shirley Hughes

The right of Shirley Hughes to be identified as author/illustrator of this work
has been asserted by her in accordance with the Copyright, Designs and Patents Act 1988

This book has been typeset in Plantin Light Educational

Printed in China

British Library Cataloguing in Publication Data:
a catalogue record for this book is available from the British Library

ISBN 978-1-4063-7275-5

www.walker.co.uk

THE NURSERY COLLECTION
NOISY

WALKER BOOKS
AND SUBSIDIARIES
LONDON • BOSTON • SYDNEY • AUCKLAND

Noisy noises!
Pan lids clashing,

Dog barking,
Plate smashing,

Telephone ringing,
Baby bawling,

Midnight cats
Cat-a-wauling,

Door slamming,

Aeroplane zooming,

Vacuum cleaner
Vroom-vroom-vrooming,

And if I dance and sing a tune,
Baby joins in with a saucepan and spoon.

Gentle noises …
Dry leaves swishing,

Falling rain,
Splashing, splishing,

Rustling trees,
Hardly stirring,

Lazy cat
Softly purring.

Story's over,
Bedtime's come,

Crooning baby
Sucks his thumb.

All quiet, not a peep,

Everyone is
fast asleep.